Zoologists in the Field

the BIG PICTURE

CAPSTONE PRESS
a capstone imprint

Louise Spilsbury

First Facts is published by Capstone Press, a Capstone imprint,
151 Good Counsel Drive, P.O. Box 669, Mankato, Minnesota 56002.
www.capstonepub.com

First published in 2010 by A&C Black Publishers Limited, 36 Soho Square, London W1D 3QY
www.acblack.com
Copyright © A&C Black Ltd. 2010

Produced for A&C Black by Calcium. www.calciumcreative.co.uk

032010
005746ACF10

Library of Congress Cataloging-in-Publication Data
Spilsbury, Louise.
  Zoologists in the field / by Louise Spilsbury.
     p. cm. — (First facts. Big picture)
  Includes index.
  ISBN 978-1-4296-5510-1 (library binding)
  ISBN 978-1-4296-5520-0 (paperback)
  1. Zoologists—Juvenile literature. 2. Animals--Research—Juvenile
literature. 3. Zoology—Vocational guidance—Juvenile literature. I.
Title. II. Series.
QL50.5.S65 2011
590.92—dc22   2010011219

Acknowledgements

The publishers would like to thank the following for their kind permission to reproduce their photographs:

Cover: Shutterstock: Tischenko Irina (front), Alle (back). **Pages:** Fotolia: Kitch Bain 21, Fabrice Beauchene 15,
Kirubeshwaran 12-13, Andrea Riva 16-17; Istockphoto: Marcel Pelletier 6-7; Shutterstock: Petrov Andrey 12, Kitch
Bain 1, Braam Collins 18-19, Lucian Coman 2-3 (background), 5, David Dea 22-23, Tiago Jorge da Silva Estima 24,
Eric Isselée 7, Kwest 4-5, Milos Markovic 20-21, Christian Musat 3, Nik Niklz 14-15, Dr. Morley Read 19, Szefei 8,
Aaron Welch 11, Brooke Whatnall 4, Worldswildlifewonders 8-9, Ximagination 16, Ludmila Yilmaz 10-11.

Contents

A Zoologist 4

At the Zoo 6

In Rain Forests 8

In Grasslands......................... 10

In Deserts 12

In Polar Places 14

In Oceans 16

In the Lab 18

Be a Zoologist 20

Glossary 22

Further Reading 23

Index 24

A Zoologist

Zoologists are people who study different animals all around the world.

All about animals

Zoologists learn about where animals live, what they eat, and how they get their food.

This zoologist is finding out about koala bears.

Cute!

Wild side

Zoologists study animals in zoos and in the wild. Some animals attack people if they feel scared. Zoologists try not to frighten them.

Sssscary!

At the Zoo

Some zoologists are zookeepers. They care for animals in zoos.

Happy animals

Zookeepers make sure animals eat healthy. They put rocks, ponds, and trees around the animals to make them feel at home.

Bathtime!

In danger

Some animals are in danger in the wild. In zoos, these animals can be well looked after and have babies. This will hopefully stop them from dying out.

Panda mothers and babies can be cared for in a zoo.

In Rain Forests

Rain forests are huge forests with very tall trees. They are found in hot and wet places.

Up high, down low

Zoologists study animals that live on the rain forest floor, such as **jaguars**. They also study birds and other animals that live up in the trees.

Colorful birds called toucans live in rain forests.

Gone forever?

Zoologists are worried about rain forest animals. A lot of rain forest trees are being chopped down. If rain forest animals lose their home, they may die out.

We need trees!

In Grasslands

Grasslands are places covered with tall grasses. Zoologists study how animals survive here.

Sneaky hunters

Animals such as lions and cheetahs have fur that blends in with grass. This helps them sneak up on **prey**, such as zebras and deer.

Can you see me?

Poop clue

One way to tell where grassland animals have been is to check out their poop! If it is fresh and smelly, it means the animal has only just left.

Animals also check out poop to tell if another animal is near.

11

In Deserts

Zoologists also visit deserts. These are the hottest places on Earth and are covered in sand.

No rain, no water?

It hardly ever rains in deserts, so zoologists study how animals here get water. Most get water from their food.

Some desert rats can turn their pee back into water. Handy!

Keeping cool

Many desert animals, such as **scorpions**, stay underground or in the shade in the day. They only come out at night, when it is cooler.

I'm cool!

13

In Polar Places

The poles are the coldest places on Earth! Zoologists study how animals here survive the cold.

It helps to be fat!

The polar bear lives in the North Pole. It has a thick layer of fat to keep it warm.

Brrrr!

Egg warming

Emperor penguins live at the South Pole. The males keep the female's eggs warm by holding them on their feet until they **hatch**.

Penguins cuddle their babies to keep them warm.

Baby

15

In Oceans

Zoologists travel in submarines, swim in diving suits, or float in cages to study ocean animals.

On the menu?

Some zoologists study what ocean animals eat and how they find their food.

Sharks hunt fish and other ocean animals for food.

Save some fish for us!

Fishy facts

Zoologists are worried about ocean animals. Fishing boats are taking too many fish from the oceans. Soon there may not be enough left for ocean animals to eat.

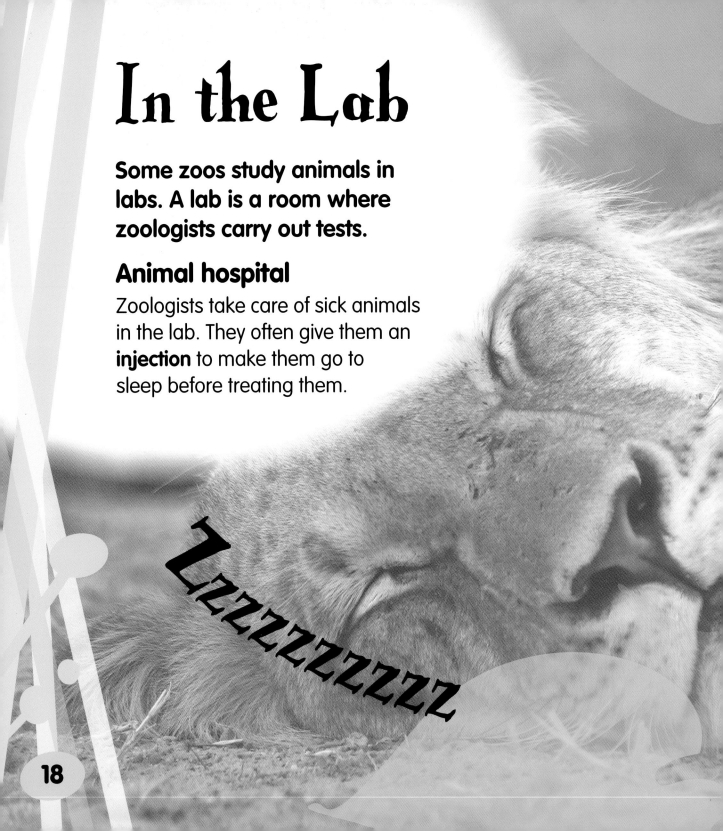

In the Lab

Some zoos study animals in labs. A lab is a room where zoologists carry out tests.

Animal hospital

Zoologists take care of sick animals in the lab. They often give them an **injection** to make them go to sleep before treating them.

Zzzzzzzzz

Small worlds

Zoologists study tiny animals in a lab, too. Some zoologists study nests of ants to find out more about how they live.

Leaf cutter ants bite off pieces of leaf to take back to the nest.

Be a Zoologist

If you love animals, you might want to become a zoologist.

Look and learn

Start to study the animals around you. Watch them in your backyard or in a park. Draw the animals and write down what they do.

Zoologists can study and help animals in the wild.

Keep it wild

If you love being outside, being a zoologist is a great job. And best of all, you can find out how to help animals everywhere.

Hang out with us!

Glossary

hatch when a baby animal breaks out of its shell

injection medicine given through a needle

jaguars large, spotted wild cats

poles places at the ends of the Earth where it is very cold. The North Pole is at the top and the South Pole is at the bottom of the Earth.

prey an animal that is caught and eaten by other animals

scorpions insects with large claws and a deadly sting in their tails

submarines boats that travel underwater

survive being able to stay alive

Further Reading

FactHound offers a safe, fun way to find Internet sites related to this book. All of the sites on FactHound have been researched by our staff.

Here's all you do:

Visit www.facthound.com

FactHound will fetch the best sites for you!

Books

DK First Animal Encyclopedia (DK First Reference Series) by Penelope Arlon, Dorling Kindersley (2004).

Animal Picture Atlas by Hazel Maskell, Usborne Publishing (2008).

National Geographic Encyclopedia of Animals by Karen McGhee and George McKay, National Geographic Society (2006).

Index

ants 19

babies 7, 15

danger 7
desert rats 12
deserts 12–13

eat 4, 6, 16

food 4, 12, 16
fur 10

grasslands 10–11

injection 18

jaguars 8

labs 18–19

oceans 16–17

penguins 15
polar bears 14
poles 14–15
poop 11
prey 10

rain forests 8–9

scorpions 13
sharks 16
survive 10

trees 9

water 12
wild animals 5, 7, 21

zookeepers 6
zoos 5, 6–7